THE Sengi AND THE Snail

AN AFRICAN FOLK TALE TOLD BY FATU ROSETTE

Illustrated by
John Vincent

AuthorHouse™ UK
1663 Liberty Drive
Bloomington, IN 47403 USA
www.authorhouse.co.uk
Phone: 0800.197.4150

Published by AuthorHouse 11/06/2018

ISBN: 978-1-7283-8010-0 (sc)
ISBN: 978-1-7283-8009-4 (e)

Print information available on the last page.

Any people depicted in stock imagery provided by Getty Images are models,
and such images are being used for illustrative purposes only.
Certain stock imagery © Getty Images.

This book is printed on acid-free paper.

Because of the dynamic nature of the Internet, any web addresses or links contained in
this book may have changed since publication and may no longer be valid. The views
expressed in this work are solely those of the author and do not necessarily reflect the
views of the publisher, and the publisher hereby disclaims any responsibility for them.

authorHOUSE®

THE CHARACTERS

Siska
A Sengi or Elephant Shrew. A small shrew with a long nose that looks a bit like a tiny elephant's trunk.

Kassongo
An African Land Snail.

Moseka
Kassongo's twin who is very clever.

Kayingo and Kabibi
Snail friends of Kassongo.

Disko the Dik Dik
A small African Antelope about thirty centimetres high.

Tchisakedee
A good natured tortoise.

Other characters include: Crane flies, Ants, Secretary birds, Dragonflies, Leopards, Anteaters, Hawks and Eagle Owls.

ONCE upon a time there was an Elephant Shrew called Siska the Sengi.. She lived in the grasslands of Central Africa. Siska spent all day running around her territory eating every insect, snail, and grub she could find. Because it was so dry her favourite food was nice juicy snails.

But there was one snail, An African Land Snail called Kassongo who was very clever and he always managed to escape being eaten. He and his equally clever friends lived under a rock which they called the Snail Room where they were sheltered, safe and out of the hot day-time sun.

THE SNAIL ROOM

THEY all had their own tricks for dealing with Siska. Kassongo, when grabbed would shout "Watch out! Hawk!" when Siska grabbed him, which scared her, as Sengies are the favourite food of hawks and many other animals and birds.

ONE morning at first light, Siska, having run three times round her territory and consumed a beetle, two crane flies, four moths and was hoping to wash them down with a nice snail, actually ran over Kassongo before realizing he was a snail not a stone. She ran so fast that she has actually gone past him before realizing she could smell his snail trail.

Quickly running back, she found him disappearing into the Snail Room.

"Good morning Siska. Are you well?" He enquired, from the safety of the snail room.

"How will I ever catch you?" Squeaked Siska, peevishly.

"By Surprise," said Kassongo who Siska longed to silence with some enjoyable chewing.

"You can run faster than me, but I can think faster than you," added Kassongo.

"Then let's have a race, Kassongo. My legs against your brain. If you can think of a way to run round my territory faster than me, I will promise not to eat you. If I win, you will be my celebration breakfast."

Siska licked her lips just imagining her triumph. From the depths of the Snail Room, Kassongo thought about the challenge. So far, his brain had triumphed over Siska's speed but eventually his reputation as 'The Snail Who Cried Hawk' would eventually cost him his life.

"Agreed," said Kassongo, "but we need a referee. I don't want you to win by eating me along the way."

"A REFEREE? Who do you suggest?" demanded Siska impatiently. She has devoured her last moth three minutes ago and was already hungry.

"How about Tchisakedee the Tortoise. He knows all about racing. A little old now but when he was young I hear he was a champion sprinter."

"That's true," agreed Siska. "I hear he ran a mile in four days."

So it was agreed. Since Kassongo couldn't go out in the heat of the day, Siska would find Tchisakedee and seek help.

While Siska left to find both food and ageing sprinters, Kassongo withdrew into his shell to conserve moisture and think about his problem.

And what a problem it was. Siska was no mastermind but where Tchisakedee had covered his mile in four days, Siska could run eight miles in an hour. He was joined in due course by various friends hurrying to snail room before the morning sun could bake them.

THEY greeted each other and were settling down for the day when Kassongo told them of his encounter with Siska and the problem of how to win a race against her.

"The hard truth is that you will not." Answered a snail called Moseka. She had survived with encounters with Siska, thanks to a talent for mimicry. A gift that enabled her to imitate creatures as different as Anteaters and Secretary Birds.

THE Secretary bird is a creature that looks like a cross between a Crane and a Road Runner and regularly includes Sengies in their diet.

"Running and eating is about all the Sengies can do. Let's see how we can help," continued Moseka.

"What about giving him a piggy back?" asked a morose snail called Kayingo. He was tired, and after a long night all he wanted was sleep, not solving the puzzle of creating a turbo-charged snail.

At this point they heard footsteps outside and the sound of a creature very much out of breath.

"Kassongo. Will you come out here, please? I want to talk about the race. Don't worry. I won't eat you. Not before I win."

Slowly and very cautiously Kassongo emerged into the sublight. The sight of Siska licking her lips was worrying, to say the least. Standing beside Siska was Tchisakedee.

HE was a little out of breath from trying to keep up with Siska. Towering above them at almost a foot tall was Disko the Dik Dik.

"**WE** need to agree the course, Kassongo. I suggest we start here and do a lap around my territory. I have a network of paths throughout it. Let me show you."

With a small claw she drew a square in the sand to represent her neighbourhood. There was a path around the perimeter which marked her border that she never crossed. All Elephant Shrews carry an accurate map of the paths in their territory in their heads. It is how they escape from their attackers.

With a precision that would be envied by a general planning a battle, she added paths and intersections. She marked the spot where The

Snail Room was situated, the route to what she called the Ring Road and the circuit they would travel. The winner would be the first back at the rock.

"I will be watching you all to ensure fair play. Disko has very kindly agreed to be transport and my viewing platform. Fair Enough?"

"Fair enough," said Kassongo.

"I CAN live with that," added Siska, confidently expecting to do so which was more than she could say for Kassongo.

"See you all at dawn, then" Squeaked Siska, unable to check the pangs of hunger and bounded off to find ants. Many ants squirt formic acid as a deterrent to being eaten. To Siska that counted as spicy food.

Kassongo returned to his friends out of the sun into the snail room. Tchisakedee decided to remain in the sun and Disko spent the day under a tree and wishing he has a refuge like a cave or sheltering rock... Something a little more substantial than just running for his life. From under the rock came the rumble of a group of snails putting their shells together to solve a knotty problem. And from thirty metres away Disko, whose hearing was excellent, could hear the crunch and rustle of a young lacewing fly, who had discovered, a little too late, that altitude is a good thing. Meeting Siska face to face like this, had that effect on young lacewing flies.

TEN hours later, as the African sun descended in the west like a vast orange balloon, Kassongo and his friends emerged from the Snail Room. They had a busy night ahead of them.

They had to find food and execute their plans. While they foraged, Siska, in her little nest was settling down to sleep. In her tummy were a lacewing fly, a beetle and a moth. In her cheek pouches, two dragon flies would hopefully suffice to keep hunger away till dawn.

Throughout the hours of darkness, they searched for food but rather than wander aimlessly around they used Siska's pathways. Back and forth they travelled until the last hour before sun up, when they look up their posts ready for Phase Two of the plan. As they headed back to the snail room some of their number were missing.

AS the sky in the east began to pale Kassongo took refuge under some grasses about the five metres from the finishing line and settled down to wait. As did a snail called Kabibi who was in a similar spot near the place where the path from the Snail Room joined the Ring Road. Further along the route, Kayingo had found a similar spot to wait. The others returned to base leaving Moseka to meet and greet Siska and the Umpires.

As the sun rose Siska stirred in her nest and swallowed the last of her dragonflies and set out for the contest. She paused to eat a fly who had chosen a bad moment to do his morning exercises.

Siska scampered to the rock and found Tchisakedee yawning noisily and Disko the Dik Dik wearing the happy expression of someone who has not been eaten by a leopard during the night. Tchisakedee was less pleased. He like to let the sun war, him up before starting to move but he was a good natured Tortoise and was also a little curious about how Kassongo would manage today.

MOSEKA, being Kassongo's twin, looked just like her brother and as she was able to mimic his voice, it made her the ideal small to start the race.

"Good morning, Siska," said Moseka who sounded like Kassongo, "How nice to see you. Are you looking forward to your new diet?"

"African Land Snail is not a new diet. I have eaten many of your friends and in about ten minutes I think I will be digesting you!" Retorted Siska.

"CHILDREN. Children." Tchisakedee rebuked.

"If you simply got me out of bed to watch you argue, I am going home."

He slowly climed onto Disko's back.

"Now are you both ready?"

Siska and, as she thought, Kassongo took their places.

"Go!" roared Tchisakedee.

A PUFF of red dust and Siska was gone. From his hiding place the real Kassongo watched contentedly as the umpires followed, leaving Moseka unobserved. Phase One of the plan had been he careful laying down of the snail trail. Phase Two was the successful substitution of Kassongo at the starting line.

Having heard the race start, the substitute Kassongo normally known as Kabibi emerged from cover and joined the path at the Ring Road. She was quickly overtaken by Siska who was thunderstruck at the sight of what she took to be Kassongo already in the lead. Siska put her head down and shot past him.

From his seat on Disko, Tchisakedee blinked at the sight of, what he took to be, Kassongo. Already in the lead. Looking back at the rock under which was the Snail Room, Moseka could not be seen. She was now at the other side of the rock ready to cheer for Kassongo in her own way. Phase Three was about to begin.

Using her talent for mimicry, Moseka's selection of the harsh "MWEAH" of an Eagle Owl could only cause alarm. This giant bird definitely included Sengies and Dik Diks on its menu. Hearing them cry, Disko shied in terror almost unseating Tchisakedee.

Siska immediately abandoned the race and dived for cover.

UP ahead the snail Kayingo heard the cue and took up the race unobserved by anyone least of all Disko or Tchisakedee. In addition to her understandable fear of being eaten, Disko was scared of flying so the sound of an Eagle Owl nearly gave her heart failure.

From her shelter Siska eventually peered out. No sign of danger. She breathed a sigh of relief. Mixed in with the breath of air was the smell of the snail trail. She rejoined the path. Yes. There it was. It actually was the smell of Kassongo who had passed that way in the night when running. If you could call it running, on part of the course.

"How is he doing this?" Squeaked a baffled Siska. She took off in what she thought was his wake but so intently was she following that she failed to notice it pveered off the main path towards one of her inner tracks and she didn't spot the mistake until she collided with a young Acacia tree. This was Phase Four. It was to lure Siska off track and there is nothing like the smell of a snail to do that.

WATCHING from on top of Disko, Tchisakedee was mystified.

"WHERE is she going?" he asked.

"Never mind where she's going. Where's that owl?" said Disko nervously.

Having realized her mistake, Siska was back on her Ring Road in no time and racing to make up lost ground.

"I am going to tear him to shreds!" she vowed, forgetting that tearing him to shreds was the whole point of this contest. Up ahead she spotted him. Actually it was Kayingo but at the speed she was moving there was no time to waste. She flew past him, convinced she could win the race have her victory confirmed and return to eat in less than a minute. The thought spurred her on.

Up ahead she spotted a beetle. It was nearly four minutes since her last meal, which for her was almost a hunger strike, so she pounced. It was only after biting happily did she realize it was the wing case of a dung beetle she had eaten yesterday.

"KASSONGO you did that deliberately!" She yelled, as she resumed the race.

Up ahead was the home straight. Approaching the last corner she was overjoyed. Behind her was the soon to be eaten Kassongo. Ahead, there was the finishing line, there were Disko and Tchisakedee arguing about the Eagle Owl, and there, to her frustration was Kassongo crossing the finishing line.

It was a baffled and furious Siska who came in second and came to a stand by what she had hoped would be breakfast. For a moment she was tempted to forget the agreement and eat him anyway, but in fairness she couldn't accuse him of cheating. She had smelled his trail back there and that trail was unbroken right up to Kassongo himself.

"What? Where? How?" She panted.

"Do you have a problem, Siska?" Enquired Kassongo, with the happy smugness of a snail who is bathing in daylight rather than Siska's stomach.

Having worked out that if there had been an Eagle Owl around it would have pounced by now Disko turned her attention to the racers.

"Well really Siska," he said. "Kassongo crossed the line first. So you cannot eat him. He won."

SISKA was bitterly disappointed at her own loss but as an animal who featured on the menus of so many creatures herself, she was sporting enough to concede.

"Congratulations, Kassongo. As agreed, I will not eat you."

"Thank you," said Kassongo, graciously.

He watched Siska bound away and pounce on a Crane Fly which had just chosen a very bad time to pause for a rest.

WITH Siska some distance away wolfing down her food, Tchisakedee turned to Kassongo.

"Well. How did you do it?"

"I have no idea what you mean." Said Kassongo evenly.

At this point, Moseka came round the corner of the rock, nodded to the assembled company, congratulated Kassongo and shuffled into the Snail Room.

"You didn't run the whole race, did you? You put your friends all along the way."

"Are you going to give me away?"

Tchisakedee thought for a moment. He was very old and had watched the drama between hunter and hunted played out many times. There could be no rule book when you are fighting for your life.

"No I am not. All you have cheated, my friend, is death. My congratulations."

"**YOU** forgot one thing, Kassongo." Said a high pitched and extremely angry voice behind them. "Sengies have excellent hearing. And thanks to *your* choice of *this* referee I now know what you did and how you did it.

If Kassongo had possessed feet he would cheerfully have kicked himself for not conducting this conversation from the safety of The Snail Room.

"I just ate a few seconds ago or I would be claiming my prize right now."

Kassongo tried to lick his lips. Suddenly his throat seemed to have gone dry. He watched Siska breathing heavily and braced himself to follow that Crane Fly.

"I will make you a new deal, my slimy friend. You were clever enough to pull off this stunt so you can do a little favour for me."

"**YES**. Anything. Please tell me." Cried Kassongo a little less smug than he had been a minute ago. "I need extra eyes. Out here we have hawks, snakes, cats and who knows what else.

You and your pals can be my sentries. Take turns to stand on top of that rock and be my sentries during the day time."

"**IN** the daytime? In the sunlight? Where birds can see me?" Queried Kassongo, plaintively.

"Of course if you prefer it we can go back to the original agreement, I will be happy to oblige," offered Siska, removing a bit of Crane Fly leg from between her teeth.

Kassongo was smart enough to realize that adaptability is the key to survival.

"Sentries it is!" Said Kassongo, breathing freely and glad to be able to do so at all. And so it worked out.

Kassongo and his friends assumed their new role as look-outs. Moseka in particular with her carrying voice was a great success. Her talent alone meant that the snails, Siska, Disko and Tchisakedee could live happily and longer ever after.

THE END

and So To Bed

Fatu Rosette was born in Isiro, in the Dem. Republic of Congo. Her father was a manager on a coffee plantation in Watsa where she was surrounded by wildlife. In her school holidays she visited her grandmother, who told her many African tales. One that captured her imagination tells of group of African Land Snails and their feud with a little Elephant Shrew who wants to eat them.

Fatu moved to the UK in 2007 where she lives with her husband and 3 children.

John Vincent, cartoonist and illustrator, was born and lives in Fowey, Cornwall.

John Vincent, cartoonist and illustrator, was born and lives in Lower Cornwall.